I Can Follow the Rules

by Molly Smith • illustrated by Julia Patton

"Anya!" I yelled across the room.

"Do you want to play with me?"

2

"Remember the rules, Eva," said Miss Jan. "Please use your inside voice."

Our Classroom Rules

1. Use your inside voice.
2. Use your walking feet.
3. Use your listening ears.
4. Take turns and share.
5. Be kind to one another.

So I ran over to talk to Anya.

"Slow down, Eva," said Miss Jan.
"Use your walking feet, please."

"Rules, rules, rules," I mumbled.

"We're not allowed to do *anything*."

"We're allowed to play dress-up," said Anya.
"Here, you can be the hero."

Anya buried herself in blocks.
"Help me, Super Eva!" she cried.

I came running super fast.
Then I tried to super-leap
over the dollhouse.

My super toe caught on the roof.
Crash! Smash!

Miss Jan came over.
"What happened?"
she asked.

11

"I was Super Eva and I was running, and then I was leaping, and then I fell," I explained.

"We want you to have lots of fun," said Miss Jan.
"But we also have rules so you will be safe."

"I'm sorry," I said. "I will follow the rules."

"I know you can!" said Miss Jan.

Then Anya gave me a big hug and
I remembered our last classroom rule.

Be kind to one another.

And that is the best rule of all.

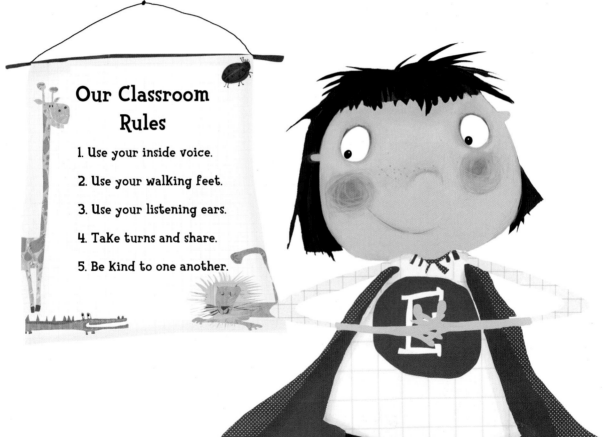

Our Classroom Rules

1. Use your inside voice.

2. Use your walking feet.

3. Use your listening ears.

4. Take turns and share.

5. Be kind to one another.